Special Thanks to our Kickstarter backers!

Maria Clapham, Cate Denial, Jayne Denial, Valerie Clapham, Lucy Arnold, Simon Melluish, Abi Gore, Grace and Ashley Wager, Sarah Wilkinson, Ste Grocock, Rob Thewlis, Sara Riley, Yvonne and Nigel Denton, Rich Madders, Dragon Steel Books, Steve Hudson, Phill and Pete Stockdale, Sarah and Chris Lowe, Tracy Marriner, Ellen Higginbottom, Hannah Parker, Barrie Ashworth, Lisa Ashworth, Jess Ashworth, Kirsty Larcombe, Jake Lane, Alex Harrison, Laura Griffin, John Gorman, Gemma Saint, Andy Denial, Wayne and Margaret Lenton, Pauline and Peter Coates, Nicola Marshall, Rachael Tyminski, Georgina Sutton, Emma Yarwood, Johanne and Will Fludgate, Nick Myers, Marilyn Taylor, Kate Worthington, Carol Harper, Alison Webb, Tanya Taylor, Lisa Bramhall, Iain Logan, Nisu Thomas, Stacey Burton, Joanne Cartmell, Sharan Ubhi, Karl Yates, Monica Leonard, Christina Cule, Kerry Swales, Tania, Rhiannon Thomas, Alicia and Jason Elberts, Kayleigh Barnett, D. Welch, Jessica Muff, Sabina Loates, Julie and Alan Johnson, Boo Thompson, Sean Twycross, Tracy Higginbottom, Ben Cann, Joanne Loftus, Katie Hawke, Adam Smith, my sister Rachel, Mark O'Shea, Chris Lockwood, Charlotte Jeal, Steve Jayne, Mark Denial, Michelle, John Dawson, Liam Rowatt, Debbie Hall, Paul Denial, Jessica Blakemore, Jane Tattersall, Darren Smith, Emma Harris, Antonia Wild, Amy Hobson, Jane-Marie Wright, David Thompson, Joanna Howard., Lynn Denial, Margaret Denial and Jai Singh Rai.

CARL MCKEOWN PUBLISHING
First Published in Great Britain in 2022 by KDP and Ingram Spark.
'The Queen Unseen' Copyright © Carl McKeown.
ISBN Paperback 9781739621308
ISBN e-book 9781739621315
Imprint Carl McKeown

All rights reserved. No part of this publication can be reproduced or copied in any form without prior permission of the publisher, nor be circulated in any form other than originally intended.
Printed in the UK.

This book is dedicated to my wife, Sarah – the power to my light.

Come along, settle down – get yourself a drink,

And I'll explain how our Queen is more fun than you'd think.

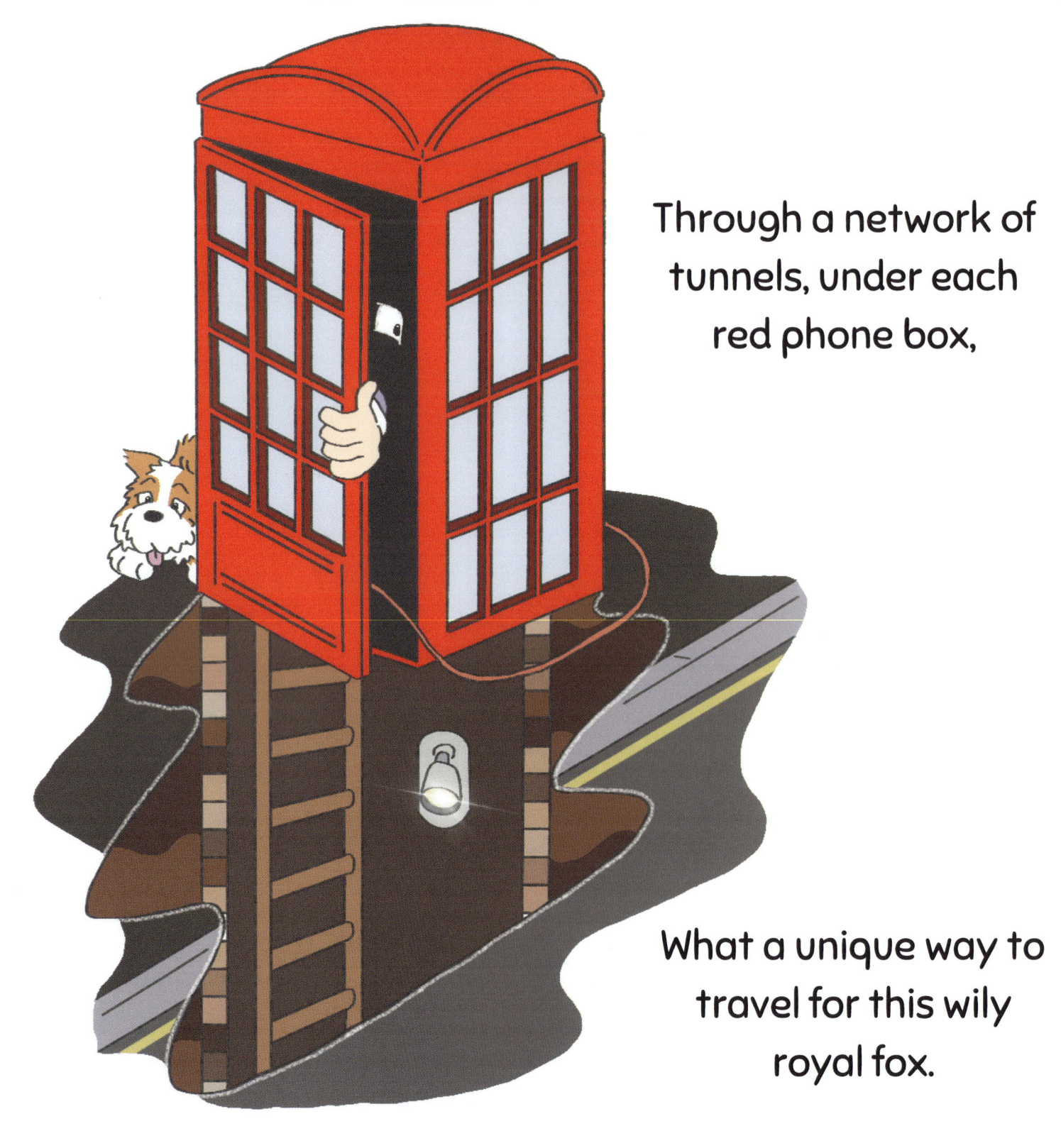

Through a network of tunnels, under each red phone box,

What a unique way to travel for this wily royal fox.

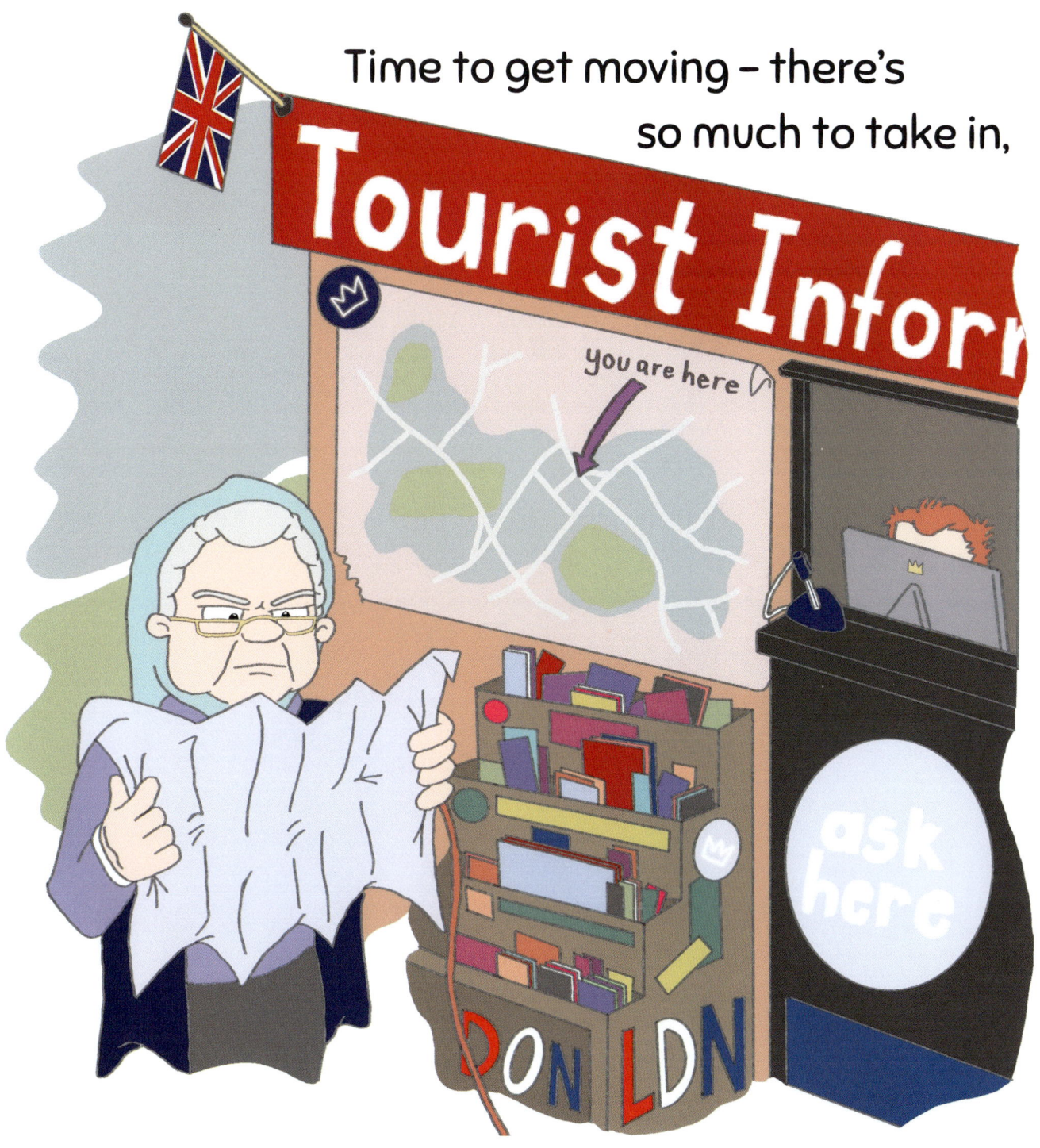

Time to get moving – there's so much to take in,

One could do with a map, to see where to begin.

Ma'am will take the tube –
the London Underground,

It's the one perfect place to avoid being found.

On the Northern or Central, but avoid Piccadilly,

One has done that before – and looked kind of silly.

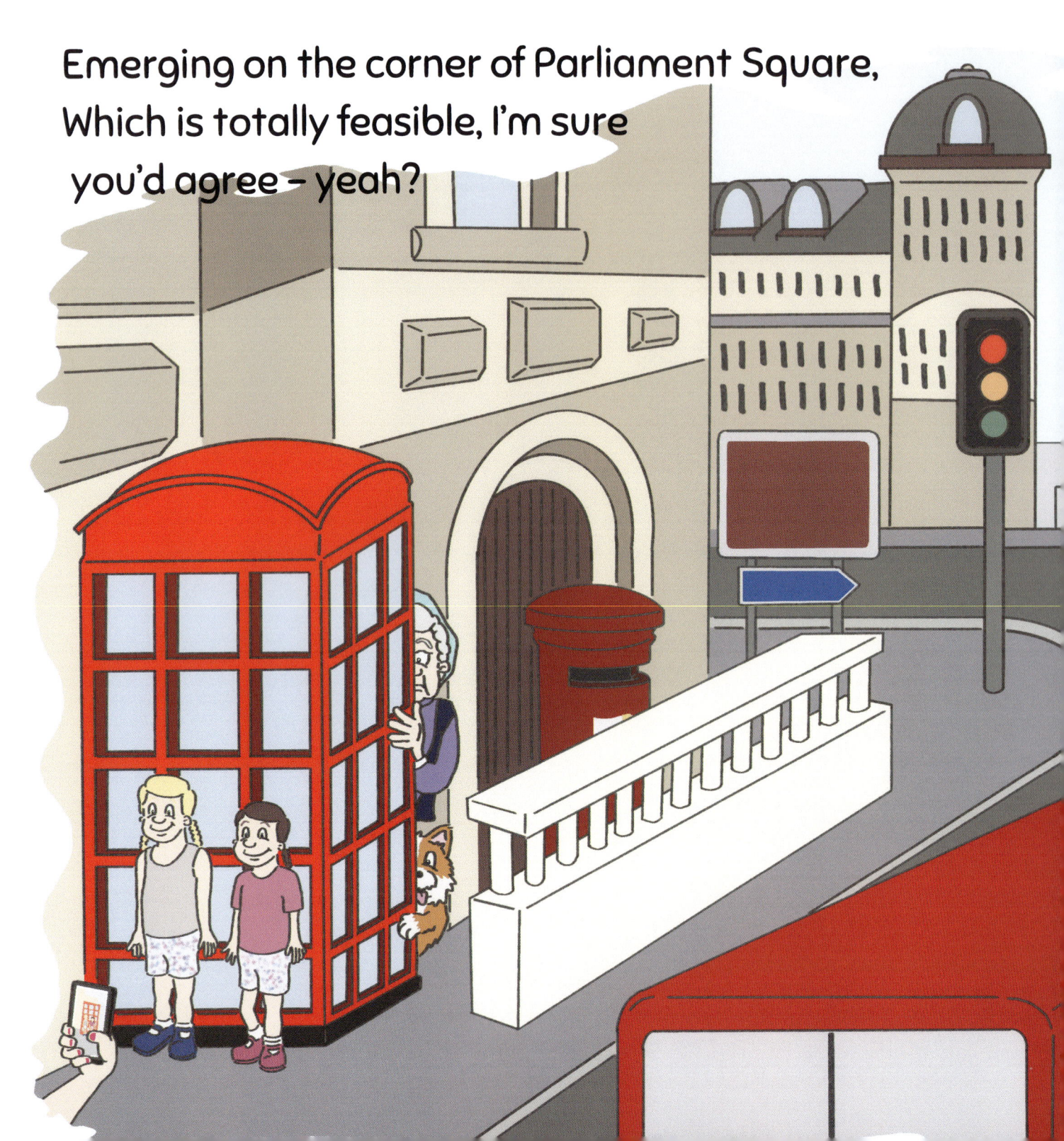

Emerging on the corner of Parliament Square, Which is totally feasible, I'm sure you'd agree – yeah?

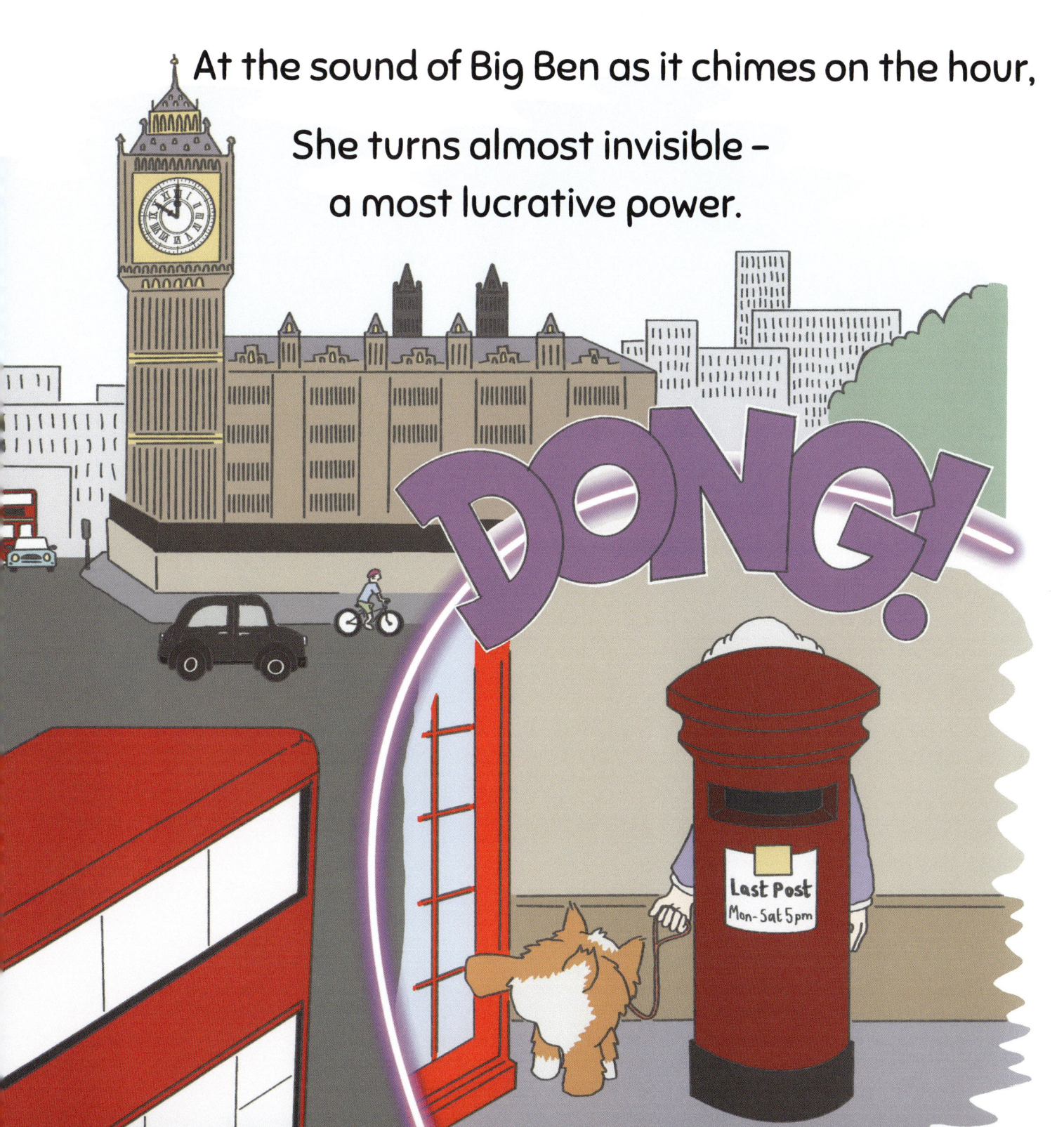

At the sound of Big Ben as it chimes on the hour,
She turns almost invisible –
a most lucrative power.

DONG!

A bedazzling display, all the Beefeaters guard,
Getting access is, quite unsurprisingly, hard.

The Crown Jewels are protected by laser alarms,

Best leave well alone so that all remains calm.

It seems ruling the country does not count for much,

But surely the Queen can at least have a touch...?

But where to go now? Are we already stuck? Because the aim's to stay hidden, if we have any luck.

I'll be honest Archaeopteryx is quite tricky to rhyme,
(ark-ee-op-ter-ix)

But there is so much to see from the 'dinosaur times'.

Some big, some small so many things catch her focus,

Nothing more than the 26 metre long Diplodocus.

Next to Leicester – which is not the last square on these travels,
In disguise – of course – so this plan doesn't unravel.

Well the nearby big theatres to be quite exact,

With the hope that shes not the one caught in the act.

So many lights, so many songs to hum,
But nowhere's more exciting than the ...

... PALLADIUM

No queues for Queenie, she's got this thing covered,
Sneaking in through the Stage Door so she's not discovered.

But she's not in the wardrobe or among all the props,

Where else would you find her –

but in the Royal Box?

With that show now over, to the secret trap door;
It's a good job the phone boxes aren't used any more.

Taking care not to stand on the rails that go 'ZAP',

While everyone else hears the words 'MIND THE GAP'.

If you're curious, Ma'am is taking the Jubilee Line,
But no drivers around – surely this is a sign...

It can't be too tricky; it's just forwards and back,
and we're off – all aboard – it's a royal tube hijack!

Then onto the museum where everyone's made from wax,
And causing some mischief's our plan of attack.

Back with the family, so let's all strike a pose,
But one has to ask ...

Dusk's now drawing in, but she's done this before,
It's a chance to tag on to the last Palace tour.

At the back of the tour group, one blends into the crowd.

Then sneaks into the throne room where no one's allowed.

And giving this adventure one last farewell kiss,

Settles down in her bedroom, like nothing's amiss...

What a journey it's been, the day's gone by so fast,
One will have to make sure this 'first' isn't her last.

Printed in Great Britain
by Amazon